that'sSO raven

2 Good 2 B True

Adapted by Alice Alfonsi
Based on the series created by
Michael Poryes
Susan Sherman
Part One is based on the teleplay written by
Dava Savel & Carla Banks Waddles
Part Two is based on the teleplay written by
Michael Feldman

Watch it on
DISNEY CHANNEL
abc Kids

DISNEY PRESS

VOLO

New York

Printed in the United States of America

First Edition
1 3 5 7 9 10 8 6 4 2

Library of Congress Control Number on file.

ISBN 0-7868-4683-6

For more Disney Press fun, visit www.disneybooks.com
Visit DisneyChannel.com

Part One

Chapter One

"Come on, *reach*," Raven Baxter urged her best friend, Chelsea Daniels. "You're so close."

"Rae, I can't do it!" wailed Chelsea.

Girl, thought Raven, don't give up on me now!

Strapped into safety harnesses, the two friends clung to a tall rock wall in the Bayside school gym. The top of the wall was only inches away.

"You can do it. Yes, you can," Raven coaxed Cheslea, who was struggling just below her. "A little bit further."

Chelsea knew Raven was counting on her. Straining, she reached up with all her strength—to hold the tube of lip gloss just a little bit higher.

"Got it!" Raven cried, pulling the applicator wand free. "Ooh, girl, Mocha Frost, my favorite." She brushed the shimmering gloss across her lips, then glanced at her classmates on the gym floor below. "Now I can look *good* coming down," she whispered to Chelsea. "See you at the bottom!"

As their entire class looked on, Raven and Chelsea made their final pull to the top of the rock wall, then rappelled down like action heroines.

When the girls reached the floor, their teacher praised their performance. No sweat, Raven thought confidently. Well, maybe a *little* sweat. She dabbed at her forehead. Thanks to Chelsea, however, her lips were looking totally fresh.

Exchanging a high five, Chelsea and Raven

strutted out of the gym to hit the showers. They slammed through the swinging doors, then suddenly stopped. Dead ahead lay a treacherous path.

"Maybe we should take the long way to the locker room," whispered Chelsea, "and avoid, you know . . ."

"The Jock Block," Raven finished for her.

"Uh-huh," said Chelsea, nervously chewing her bottom lip.

The Jock Block, also known as the Highway of Hotties, was a short strip of hallway lined with lockers that belonged to the members of Bayside's basketball, football, and baseball teams.

Raven looked over at the twenty or so good-looking Bayside Barracudas who were talking and laughing in the corridor. She had to agree with Chelsea. "There is no way that I'm walking through *all that* looking like *all this*,"

Raven whispered, tugging at her gym clothes. Her uniform was damp with perspiration, ridiculously oversized, and an embarrassingly bright shade of yellow.

"I know," replied Chelsea. "I mean, my hair's all a mess, I'm, like, really sweaty, and, FYI, you kind of smell a little. . . . Well, actually, you smell a *lot*."

Raven frowned, raised her arm and sniffed. Okay, so her dandelion yellow sweatshirt didn't smell as fresh as a daisy, she thought, but it wasn't *that* bad. With hands on her hips, she glared at Chelsea.

"Just keepin' it real, Rae," Chelsea said, crossing her arms in the lamest hip-hop pose Raven had ever seen. "Keepin' it real."

Dang, thought Raven, I hook up my country friend with some homey lingo, and *this* is my payback. "Hey, Chelsea," she snapped, "I taught you that phrase. Don't use it against me."

Just then, the girls noticed their best friend, Eddie Thomas, coming toward them—well, actually, *hobbling* toward them—from the other end of the Jock Block. He was wearing green cargo pants, a long sweater, and a white bandage on his right foot. He struggled with a pair of crutches as he made his way down the hall.

"Look, Eddie hurt his foot," said Chelsea.

"*And* it's rock-climbing week in gym," Raven pointed out.

"Think there's a connection?" asked Chelsea.

Raven arched one eyebrow. Eddie had never been very fond of heights. Whenever they went to the mall, he refused to go *near* the glass elevators. And during last year's rock-climbing week at Bayside, Eddie had been absent every day. He claimed he'd had to attend his Uncle Fredo's funeral in Kansas

City—but Raven was pretty sure Eddie didn't even *have* an Uncle Fredo.

The girls eyed Eddie's bandaged foot and crutches suspiciously. "Hmmm," they both said, putting their fingers to their chins.

"Watch this," Raven whispered to Chelsea. Cupping her hands around her freshly Mocha-Frosted lips, she shouted, "Hey, Eddie! There's free pizza in the cafeteria!"

"Free pizza!" Eddie cried.

He picked up his crutches and began to hurry down the hall. As soon as he saw Raven laughing, however, he realized he'd been played. He slid to a stop and slowly lifted his bandaged foot—the one he'd just been running on.

"Um, what I meant to say was . . . *ow*," he told them, as he put the crutches back under his arms.

Shaking her head, Raven replied, "Eddie, it's a wall. Climb it."

"Hey, I don't do heights, okay?" Eddie informed her. "Birds gotta fly, fish gotta swim, and Eddie's gotta stay on the ground."

"Come on, Eddie," Chelsea said brightly, "you're good in every other sport. Basketball, baseball . . ."

"Again, all on *the ground*!" he pointed out.

Suddenly, Raven froze. As the world around her blurred, a scene from the future shimmered into focus. . . .

**Through her eye
The vision runs
Flash of future
Here it comes—**

I see the school gym. Hey, the rock wall is still up. Guess whatever I'm seeing is going to happen this week.

Now I see some guy climbing the wall.

Wait—I cannot believe what I'm seeing! It's Eddie! He's almost there—now he's at the top. He reaches out and smacks the coach's "victory" button, beaming as the siren and red light go off.

All right, Eddie! You're the man!

My boy looks so happy. "I made it!" he shouts, as he pumps his fist in victory.

When Raven came out of her vision, her face broke into a wide grin.

"Eddie, I just saw you climbing the wall," she told him. "You're going to make it all the way to the top!"

"Really?" asked Eddie.

Raven nodded.

"You know what this means?" asked Eddie.

Raven and Chelsea shook their heads.

Eddie dropped his crutches and raised his palms to the ceiling. "Glory! I'm healed! I can walk!" he declared with more theatrical flair than a revival-tent preacher. He gave Raven a huge grin. "I *love* that my best friend is psychic!"

Twenty minutes later, Eddie was clinging to the rock wall in the gym. He'd only managed to climb a few feet up before stark terror had gripped him and he'd squeezed his eyes shut. Below him, every single guy in his class was doubled over with laughter.

"What's the matter, Eddie?" yelled one of the jocks. "Afraid of heights?"

Through tightly clenched teeth, Eddie muttered, "I *hate* that my best friend is psychic!"

Chapter Two

"Eddie, I said I was sorry," Raven said a short time later.

Raven and Chelsea had heard about Eddie's freak-out on the rock wall. The story was all over school in no time. When they caught up with him in the hallway, Eddie was off-the-charts furious.

"Can't you just forget it?" Raven pleaded. "I mean, everybody else has."

Just then, they turned a corner. As soon as they saw him, a half dozen boys from Eddie's gym class threw themselves against their lockers, then pretended to hang there helplessly.

"Help me! I'm frozen with fear!" one kid cried.

"I need my mommy!" another squealed.

Eddie gritted his teeth, but tried to play it cool. "That is so funny," he cried to the boys, slapping his knee and pretending to laugh. He knew he'd look even more foolish if he didn't go along with their joke. "You all sound just like me. On the real!"

Eddie kept up the fake laughing until all the guys were out of earshot. Then he stopped smiling and glared at Raven. "See what you did," he snarled. Turning his back, he banged open his locker and yanked out his books.

As Raven's shoulders sagged, Chelsea jumped between her friends. "You know, Eddie," she said, "on the bright side, after this week, wall-climbing week will be over, and then everyone will forget about it and stop teasing you. You know . . . until *next* year."

Eddie sighed.

But Raven latched onto something Chelsea

had said—after all, the week wasn't over yet.

"That's right, Eddie," said Raven. "Look, they're not taking the wall down until tomorrow. That's when I must've seen you climb it. In gym *tomorrow*."

Eddie's scowl faded when he realized that Raven was right. He stared into the distance as he imagined himself ringing the coach's "victory" buzzer at the top of the wall with every last kid at Bayside cheering him on. Now, *that* would be tight, thought Eddie. Once he conquered the rock wall, he'd be cured of his fear of heights for good. He was sure of it. Then the sky would be the limit: Denali, Mount Everest . . . even the glass elevator at the Bayside Mall!

"All right! That's great," he told Raven. "After tomorrow, the whole school will know Eddie Thomas is no wimp!"

Eddie turned, finally feeling good. Just then, he noticed three more jocks down the hall. They were laughing, pointing, and clinging to their lockers in mock terror.

"Until then," Eddie added quietly, "I think I'm going to take the back way to class."

After Eddie headed down the hall, Raven turned to Chelsea and sighed with relief. "Give it up for the vision," she said, and the two did their girlfriend handshake, with knocking fists, clasping hands, and a "Bam!" on the end of it.

Suddenly, Raven was giving it up for the vision *again*! As the world froze around her, a window onto the future cracked open. . . .

**Through her eye
The vision runs
Flash of future
Here it comes—**

I see the Jock Block. As usual, the boys are looking fine!

Hey, what's this? Every last hottie is turning to stare at someone. It's a girl, and she's strutting down Hottie Highway like she's on a catwalk.

She does look stylin' in those black lace-up boots, a denim skirt, a plum cashmere half-sweater, and—hey, wait a second! Those clothes and boots look awfully familiar. . . .

I can't believe this one! It's Chelsea—and she's wearing my clothes instead of her preppy rags. She's flipping her long red hair and soaking up the attention like a finalist in a beauty pageant. It's incredible! Every jock on the block is turning his head to watch her walk past, and their jaws are actually dropping!

You go, girl!

"Girl, I just had the best vision about you!" Raven told Chelsea when she came out of her psychic trance. "I saw you walking down Jock Block looking fine, and all eyes were on you."

"Really? Wow! You mean *I have got it going on*?" Chelsea said, doing a little disco-era bump with her hips.

Once again, Raven winced at Chelsea's clueless delivery of homeboy flow.

"Hey, Chelsea," she said, biting her cheek to keep from laughing, "did I teach you that line?"

"Yeah," said Chelsea.

"Oh, well," Raven said with a shrug, "we're just going to have to work on that one as well. Come on."

chapter Three

When the school day was over, Raven headed home with Chelsea in tow. *For my vision to come true, I've got some stylin' to do!* Raven said to herself. *First stop, my closet!*

"So, where did your folks go again?" asked Chelsea as they walked into the Baxter's kitchen.

"Jamaica," replied Raven. "They're on their third honeymoon."

"Gosh, that's so romantic," Chelsea said with a dreamy sigh.

"No, it's not," said Raven. "On their second honeymoon, we ended up with my brother. *Ew.*"

"Do you like having your grandma around?" Chelsea asked.

"Oh, yeah, she's cool. But don't call her grandma. 'Cause she always says, 'Cookie, as long as I got my own teeth and my butt's still higher than my knees, no one calls me grandma.'"

Just then, the doors to the living room swung open and two figures bounded in, each holding a toy laser sword.

"All right, come on, give it up, little man," said the stylish woman in her sixties, swishing her glowing blue sword.

"Never!" shouted Raven's little brother, Cory, parrying with his red sword.

"I'm gonna touché your tushy!" cried the older woman.

Chelsea's eyes widened. "That's your *grandma*?" she asked Raven.

"Hey, I heard that!" cried Raven's grandmother. She slammed her sword on the counter right next to Chelsea, who jumped back in surprise. "Don't use that kind of language around here. It's *Vivian.*"

"Hey, Viv!" called Raven.

"Hey, Cookie!" Vivian clashed her sword with Cory's a few more times and then announced, "Fight's over, little man."

Putting down her toy sword, Vivian straightened the jacket of her leopard-print pantsuit, smoothed the collar of her lilac-colored blouse, and kissed Raven hello. Turning back to Cory, she asked, "Did you work up an appetite?"

"Yep!" declared Cory.

"Good," said Vivian, pointing toward a covered silver platter on the counter, "'cause I whipped you up something special."

Cory licked his lips. The platter was huge, and he was sure whatever was under there was going to be tasty. Slowly, his grandmother lifted the heavy lid. Cory leaned forward eagerly—then he jumped back in shock. Sitting on the platter, surrounded by pretty green garnishes, was a shriveled human head!

"Say hello to your Great Uncle Earl," Vivian said with a cackle. Then she winked at her grandson. "Gotcha!"

Cory almost laughed at the disgusting fake head but quickly caught himself. From his point of view, this was serious stuff. *He* was the kid here. *She* was the grown-up. *He* was the one who was supposed to be playing tricks on *her.*

Grandma, you are upsetting the natural order of the universe! Cory thought in outrage. "You wait," he threatened, "I'm gonna get you back."

"Well, bring it on, little man. Bring it on!" Vivian replied with a grin.

Raven rolled her eyes. One thing her grandmother could never be accused of was acting too mature. "Hey, Viv," said Raven, "I want you to meet my *bestest* friend, Chelsea."

"Oh, nice to meet you, Chelsea," said Vivian, shaking her hand.

"Yeah," said Raven, "she has a date with destiny."

"Well, a date's a date," said Vivian. She looked at Chelsea's thick turtleneck sweater and brown tartan skirt, then shook her head. "Honey, we've got to get you out of that plaid and into something *bad*," she said, reaching into her big bag on the kitchen counter. "*Voilà!*" she cried as she pulled out a ruby red sequined gown.

Dang, thought Raven, either Viv is carrying around her dry cleaning or her babysitting plans include a trip to Las Vegas.

"Wow!" said Chelsea, impressed. "All my grandma carries in her purse are old mints and used tissues."

"Well, you never know when they're gonna ask you to put on a *show*," said Vivian, singing the last few words like a pop diva. Unfortunately, the last note she hit was so high it shattered the vase on the kitchen table. Broken glass and yellow daffodils flew everywhere.

Vivian gave a "whoops, my bad!" shrug. But Raven had a hunch her grandmother was just warming up.

After they cleaned up the mess, Raven, Chelsea, and Vivian headed up to Raven's House of Design—also known as Raven's bedroom. A sewing machine, a dressmaker's dummy, and piles of funky clothes and accessories cluttered her room.

"Okay, time to get you dressed," Raven told Chelsea. She dug through her shoe stash and held up a pair of pointy-toed boots with spike heels.

"Do you like these?" asked Raven.

"Oh, I love those!" exclaimed Chelsea, reaching for them.

Raven tugged them back. "Good," she said, setting them aside. "I think I wanted to wear these tomorrow." Raven pulled out a pair of high black lace-up boots. "*These* are the ones I saw you in, girl. The Jock Block is gonna love them."

"Well, wait a minute," Vivian interrupted. "How about a hat?" She pulled an old-fashioned wide-brimmed pink bonnet from her big bag and slapped it on Chelsea's head.

Raven rolled her eyes. That fashion relic would be perfect, she thought, if I were getting Chelsea ready for an Easter parade.

"I wore this little number when I sang for the troops," Vivian informed the girls.

"Wow! The army?" asked Chelsea.

"Nope. The Cub Scouts," said Vivian. "I was one hot-looking den mother." Her eyes glazed over and she began to do a little soft shoe, remembering a routine from decades past.

"Hey, Viv," Raven said, snapping her fingers, "come back! I've gotta get Chelsea into a fly outfit."

"I love when Raven has her visions about me," said Chelsea, admiring herself in the big pink hat.

"Oh, I remember when she was a baby," said Vivian.

Raven frowned. *Oh no*, she thought, not the baby stories. *Please* not the baby stories!

"She used to stop and stare into space with this real serious look on her face," Vivian continued.

"Oh, she was having one of her visions?" asked Chelsea.

"Nope, taking a poop!" said Vivian. "Her vision face was more like this." She made a pouty face, and Raven winced with embarrassment.

"Hey, Viv," said Raven.

"What?" asked her grandmother.

"Sharing time is over." Raven handed Chelsea a skirt from her closet. "What do you think of this?"

Just then, Raven's little brother sneaked into the room. Very quietly, he placed a whoopee cushion on a nearby stool and tossed a blanket over it.

"Viv," he said, stepping up to her, "you look tired. Come, sit." With an innocent smile, Cory gestured to the blanket-covered stool.

"Oh, honey, that is so sweet," said Vivian, "but I think I'm gonna ah-ah-ah—" She reached into her bag and pulled out a wad of tissues. "*Ah-choo!*"

Cory fell back as something long and stringy came shooting out of the tissues and covered him from head to foot. *Silly String,* he realized. His grandma had hidden Silly String in her purse!

Without thinking, he backed away from the spraying string and collapsed right on the seat of the stool behind him. *PHLBBBT!* The whoopee cushion let out an obnoxious sound.

Vivian winked. "Gotcha!" she hollered.

Chapter Four

"**W**hat is taking you so long?" asked Raven, bursting into the girls' bathroom at school the next day.

"Lacing these boots," complained Chelsea. "Next time, could you buy some with zippers?"

"Okay, maybe this will help you move a little faster," said Raven. "I was just walking down Jock Block, and I have three words for you: Look. Ing. Good!" With three snaps of her fingers, Raven was gone again, bolting out of the girls' bathroom and down the hall. She wanted the long view of Hottie Highway when Chelsea walked down it.

Back inside the bathroom, Chelsea glanced at herself in the mirror. I guess I *am* looking pretty hot in Raven's clothes, she thought. If only I could get these boots laced up!

"Must. Get. On. Boots," she chanted as she struggled with the laces. Unfortunately, Chelsea was in such a hurry to finish, she hooked the lace on the right boot around a hook on the left one. Standing up, she lost her balance and began to flail around the bathroom.

She saved herself from crashing to the floor by throwing herself into an open stall. *Phew*, that was close, she told herself, collapsing onto the toilet seat.

Meanwhile, in the hallway, Eddie had already started his own strut down the Jock Block. "Yeah, you thought Jordan's comeback was big?" he told the guys who'd been teasing him the day before. "Well, in five minutes, Eddie Thomas is climbing that wall again. Read all about it."

He handed out dozens of homemade flyers advertising his second attempt to climb Bayside's version of Mount Everest.

"Thomas," said one of the jocks, "you sure you want an *audience* for this?"

"You bet he does," Raven declared, walking over to back him up. "Does this look like a man who can't take on a challenge?" she asked, sounding like a prime-time fight promoter.

"That's his head," said a second jock, pointing to Eddie's flyer, "but that's *not* his body."

Raven took a closer look at the flyer in the boy's hand. It read—

> ### EDDIE THOMAS CLIMBING THE ROCK WALL AT 1 P.M. BE THERE!

The image on the poster was a digitally designed freak with Mr. Universe's body and Eddie's face.

"Well, does that look like the *head* of a man who can't take on a challenge?" Raven said, changing her tune.

"Yeah!" cried Eddie. "Uh . . . what she said."

The two jocks just shrugged and walked off, shaking their heads doubtfully.

Raven turned to Eddie. "I'm so proud of you," she told him. "No fear of heights is gonna keep my boy down. You know what, I'll be there as soon as Chelsea's finished. Good luck."

"I don't need it—as long as I got my psychic friend," said Eddie. Then he gave Raven a hug.

Happily, Raven watched Eddie head for the boys' locker room. Thank goodness my visions gave me kickin' predictions for my friends, thought Raven. One bud down, one to go!

Just then, she noticed Chelsea approaching the other end of Hottie Highway. The Chelsea Show was about to begin! As Raven watched, her best girlfriend pulled the elastic band from her ponytail and let her silky red hair fall down past her shoulders. Some of the guys in Jock Block were already turning to look.

Oh, yeah, keep it going, girl! Raven thought.

Chelsea didn't disappoint. She started her walk down the Jock Block with the self-assured strut of a true diva. Raven gave her a thumbs-up for encouragement and Chelsea fluffed her hair and sashayed with even more attitude.

Ooh, this is just like my vision! Raven thought, getting the chills. Each guy Chelsea passed turned to stare. Jaws were dropping, and all eyes were on her. One boy even blew her a kiss!

Finally, Chelsea reached the end of the Jock

Block. Raven was grinning from ear to ear. Then Chelsea spun to face the guys one more time, and Raven saw it—the reason why all eyes were glued to her best friend. Stuck to the back of Chelsea's skirt was a paper toilet-seat cover. And Chelsea had absolutely no clue.

Just as Chelsea was about to take a second run up the hall, Raven threw her arm around her neck. "How about a little *walk*?" she suggested. Applying a hold worthy of a professional wrestler, Raven yanked Chelsea down the hall and around the corner.

"What are you doing? Their eyes were glued to me!" Chelsea cried, after Raven finally let her go.

"Yeah," said Raven, "and, um, so was *that*."

"What?" asked Chelsea.

Raven pulled the toilet seat cover from the back of Chelsea's skirt and held it up. A look of complete horror crossed Chelsea's face.

"Okay," she told Raven, "um, *please* tell me you just put this there."

"Girl, you know you look hot—" Raven gulped. "From the *front*."

Chelsea squeezed her eyes shut in humiliation. When she opened them again, she was looking for a target. "How could you do this, Rae? That was the Jock Block. Thanks a lot."

Raven felt terrible. "But it's not my fault," she said. "Chelsea, it's these stupid visions. They keep messing everybody up. First, it's Eddie, now you—"

Raven suddenly stopped. She'd just remembered Eddie's "Rock Climbing Challenge." He had distributed flyers to half the school! "Oh no, Eddie. *Eddie*!" she cried, taking off down the hall.

Inside the Bayside gymnasium, Eddie clung to the rock wall only a few feet from the ground, paralyzed with fear. The scene looked pretty much like it had the day before—the only difference was this time there were a lot more spectators. A huge mob of kids had crowded in from the hallways to watch. The jocks were cracking jokes, and the other kids were screaming with laughter.

With Chelsea right behind her, Raven pushed her way through the crowd. "Eddie?" she called in a tiny voice.

"*Raven*," Eddie answered in a furious one.

"All right, you guys, break it up," Chelsea announced, waving her hands at the crowd. "There's nothing left here to see. Move on. Move on."

When Chelsea grabbed hold of Eddie's safety rope to help him down, Raven stepped up beside her. "Here, let me help you," she said.

"No, I'll do it," snapped Chelsea, working the rope by herself to lower Eddie to the floor. "I think you already 'helped' enough."

"Man, I'm the biggest joke in the school now," said Eddie when his feet touched down. He turned to face Raven, his eyes burning with anger. "Your visions are wack. Why can't you just be . . ."

"Normal?" said Raven, finishing the sentence for him. Devastated that her friends had turned on her, she turned on them—and ran out of the gym.

Chapter Five

Later, after Raven had given her friends time to cool off, she went looking for them. She found them sitting together at the bottom of a staircase.

"Hi," said Raven tentatively. "You know, I was looking for you guys in the cafeteria, and then I thought, where would two people who hate me go? And here you are. These must be the 'hate me' stairs." Eddie and Chelsea just looked at her coldly. Raven gulped. "And *those* must be the hate me *stares*."

Raven waited for Eddie and Chelsea to give her some kind of reaction—a smile, a shrug, a blink. She'd take anything. "Get it?" Raven prompted. "The hate me *stairs*. And the hate me *stares.*" Their stony expressions didn't change.

"Right," Raven said with a sigh. In the silence that followed, she sat down next to them. "You guys, look, what am I supposed to do? Should I not tell you my visions anymore? Go on some sort of psychic strike or something?"

Two jocks walked by. When they noticed Chelsea, they both ripped paper from their notebooks, turned around, and held it against their behinds. Then they laughed hysterically at their own joke.

Humiliated yet again, Chelsea turned to Raven. "Sounds good to me," she snapped.

"Yeah. No more visions," barked Eddie. He thought for a second and added, "*Unless* a piano's about to fall on my head. Then you can tell me—" He stopped talking when he noticed Chelsea looking at him like *she* would like to drop a piano on his head. "Or," he said nervously, "you can just keep it to yourself."

"Okay," said Raven. She was ready to agree to anything that would get her best friends to like her again. "So, starting today, I will no longer tell you my visions. Friends?" Raven held up her fist.

Eddie and Chelsea glanced at each other. "Friends," they agreed at last, knocking their fists with hers.

"I love you all," Raven reminded them. Relieved, she headed off to her next class.

After Raven was gone, Eddie turned to Chelsea and frowned.

"If I get hit by a piano," he told her, "I'm blaming you."

Later that day, Raven attended the school choir auditions with Chelsea.

"Okay, I'm next," Chelsea told Raven, when

her turn came. She glanced nervously at the three teachers sitting behind a table at the front of the room. A fourth teacher sat at the piano. All four teachers adjusted their glasses as they waited for Chelsea to hand over her sheet music.

"Which one do you think I should sing?" Chelsea asked Raven, showing her the two pieces. "This one I always sing," she explained, "and this other one has that really high note that Vivian helped me with."

Suddenly, Raven felt that familiar psychic tingling. As the world blurred around her, a vision of the future gave Raven a clue *which* of the two selections would be a disaster for her friend. When the vision ended, she found Chelsea staring at her, waiting for advice.

"I think . . ." Raven began.

"Go for the high note, right?" Chelsea asked excitedly.

"Uh . . ." Raven was torn. She wanted to warn Chelsea, but she'd made a promise to stop telling her friends her visions. "Your choice," Raven finally said.

With an excited nod, Chelsea gave the more difficult piece of music to the pianist. Then she introduced herself to the judges. "Hi. Chelsea Daniels."

At the piano, the teacher began to play, and Chelsea started to sing "Amazing Grace."

Raven held her breath, waiting for the high note. *It's coming, it's coming, it's coming*, she thought with dread. Then, finally, it came.

Chelsea flubbed the pitch, screeching far too high. Unfortunately, more than her voice cracked. The piano player's glasses cracked, too. And so did the glasses on all three of the teachers who were judging Chelsea's audition.

The teachers glared at Chelsea, who turned to glare at Raven.

Just like my vision, Raven thought guiltily. The one I *didn't* warn Chelsea about.

An hour later, Eddie sat in the front row of music class, holding his trombone. Raven sat next to him, holding her silver triangle. The music teacher stood at the front of the class, holding his baton.

Suddenly, Raven opened her eyes wide. A vision of the future flashed through her mind. "Hey, Eddie?" she whispered urgently when she came out of her trance.

"Yeah?" he asked.

Raven was about to warn him what she'd seen, but once again she remembered her promise. Her shoulders sagged. "Never mind," she said dejectedly.

Mr. Churnin tapped his baton. All the kids raised their instruments and began to play "Stars and Stripes Forever."

Raven held her breath. She knew what was going to happen. *It's coming, it's coming, it's coming*, she thought with dread. Then, finally, it came.

Eddie extended his arm, sending the slide of the trombone all the way out in front of him. When the slide came back, something else came with it—his teacher's toupee. It dangled from the end of Eddie's trombone like a furry animal.

Looking very bald and very angry, Mr. Churnin glared at Eddie. Eddie glared at Raven.

But I *wanted* to warn you, she thought with a sigh. Yet again, Raven felt like she'd let a friend down.

That evening, Raven found herself sitting inside a tent with her grandmother. Crickets chirped around them as Vivian speared a marshmallow with a stick.

"Ah, there's nothing like roasting marshmallows over a campfire," said Vivian.

Raven rolled her eyes. The so-called campfire was a bare lightbulb—Vivian had removed the shade from a lamp. The tent was pitched in the middle of the Baxters' living room rug.

"Hey, come on, Cookie. Smile," said Vivian. "You used to like camping in the living room when you were little. What's going on, kid?"

Holding her head in her hands, Raven groaned. "Can we talk about it later?"

"Sure!" said her grandmother. She waited five seconds, looked at her watch, and announced, "It's later." Handing Raven a skewered marshmallow, she commanded, "Now talk."

"It's these visions. I hate them," said Raven, as the two roasted their marshmallows over the lightbulb.

"I know exactly how you feel," said Vivian.

Raven shook her head. She'd never felt this down before. "No one knows how I feel," she told her grandmother. "Not even my friends. Sometimes I feel like some kind of *freak* or something."

"Do you feel like if you tell your friends your visions and it doesn't work out, that it's all your fault?" asked Vivian. "And if you don't tell them and bad stuff happens, it's still your fault? And more than anything, you wish you were just *normal*?"

Raven stared at her grandmother in amazement. "That's exactly how I feel. But I've never told anybody. How could you know?" A second later, Raven guessed. "Grandma, are you psychic?"

"Well, I don't know who this 'grandma' person is." Vivian grinned. "But Viv is. How do you think I knew what Cory was up to with his whoopee cushion? As a matter of fact, he's on his way downstairs with a couple of water balloons." Turning her head, she shouted, "Cory! Don't even think about it!"

Halfway down the staircase, Cory froze, his hands clutching three bulging water balloons. "Oh, man," he complained. With the surprise attack foiled, he was forced to retreat back to his bedroom. Busted by Grandma *again*, Cory thought in disgust. This is just *wrong*!

On the living-room floor, Raven sighed. "I wish I could just stay in this tent forever and never come out."

"Been there," Vivian confessed. "That is not the answer—"

Suddenly, the crickets stopped chirping. "Just a minute," Vivian told Raven. She opened a cassette player next to her, flipped the tape, and hit the PLAY button. The cricket sounds resumed.

"Gotta have my sound effects," Vivian explained. Then she smiled and took Raven's hand. "You know, Cookie, being psychic is a gift. It's what makes us special. And you're a lucky girl to have friends you can share it with."

"Yeah," said Raven, still not convinced, "but if I keep sharing, I'm not going to have any friends."

Vivian put a hand on Raven's shoulder and looked her straight in the eye. "Cookie," she said in a firm voice, "good friends don't go away that easy."

In her heart Raven knew her grandmother was right. Chelsea and Eddie were exactly the sort of friends Vivian was talking about: *good* ones.

Raven hugged her grandmother. "Thanks," she said.

"For what, sweetie?" asked Vivian.

"For telling me that you're psychic," Raven said. "Now I know I'm not the only one."

"And if you ever need to talk, you can always call," Vivian reminded her. "Of course, I'll know it's you calling before I pick up."

"'Cause you'll have a vision?" asked Raven.

"No, I got caller ID," Vivian replied. "Get with the program, kid. Now, answer that phone."

What phone? Raven was about to ask. Just then, it rang. "Hello?" she said, flipping open her cell. "What? Okay, okay, I'll be right there." Hanging up, Raven jumped to her feet.

"What's wrong?" Vivian asked worriedly.

Raven arched an eyebrow. "And you call yourself a psychic," she said.

Chapter Six

Bursting through the doors of the school gymnasium, Raven and Chelsea found Eddie strapped into a harness, scaling the rock wall. He had managed to climb several feet from the floor. Now he clung to the wall just two feet from the top!

"Eddie!" cried Raven. "What are you doing up there?"

"Well, I think I'm climbing a wall. But I got my eyes shut," he told her.

Earlier, Chelsea had heard a rumor that Eddie was heading for the school gym. That's when she'd called Raven. Now the girls held their breath, watching as their best friend faced his worst fear.

"Okay, I'm gonna open my eyes now," Eddie told them. Slowly he lifted his lids. "Yep, I'm on a wall!" His entire body stiffened in terror.

"Eddie, who are you doing this for?" cried Chelsea. "Everybody's gone home."

"I don't care, Chels. I'm doing it for me," Eddie declared.

"Eddie be careful. Go slowly, okay," called Chelsea.

"Okay," promised Eddie. Gritting his teeth and keeping his eyes focused upward, he reached with one hand, then another. He lifted one foot, then another. Slowly, carefully, Eddie made it to the top.

"You're doing it!" cried Raven.

"You got it!" cheered Chelsea.

There was only one thing left to do. Eddie reached out and slapped the coach's "victory" buzzer. The siren and flashing light went off.

"I made it!" Eddie shouted with pride.

"Yeah, now come down!" Chelsea called nervously.

"That was good, that was good, you guys. That was my vision!" Raven exclaimed.

"Yeah, and I *love* your visions!" Eddie told her with a triumphant grin. "Love 'em, love 'em, love 'em!" For the first time, Eddie looked down. "Man, you guys sure are tiny. Ahhhhhh!"

Losing his balance, Eddie fell backward off the wall. The safety harness caught him, but he couldn't get back on the wall. He was stuck flailing around in midair!

The girls raced over to help him. But before they could grab the rope, Eddie flipped upside down!

"Just stay right there!" cried Raven.

"We're coming up!" promised Chelsea.

By now, the girls were pros at the rock-climbing drill. They strapped into safety harnesses and crawled up the wall in record time. When they reached Eddie, Raven grabbed one arm and Chelsea grabbed the other.

The girls began to climb higher while holding his arms. If all went well, they would easily flip him right side up again. But all *didn't* go well. In the process of turning Eddie right side up, Raven and Chelsea flipped themselves upside down!

"This is way better," said Eddie, looking around.

Maybe for *you*! Raven thought.

"Okay, guys, listen," she said as the blood rushed to her head. "The trick is to stay calm."

Eddie didn't seem to hear her. He flapped his arms and legs, trying to help Raven and Chelsea. In no time, the three friends were tangled together in a rock-climbing mess.

Finally, Eddie felt something hard under his foot. He pushed down on it to steady himself.

"I'm okay," he declared, "as long as I stand on this rock thing."

Unfortunately for Chelsea, that "rock thing" was the safety helmet on her *head*!

At last, Raven managed to flip herself upright, swing toward the wall, and grab hold. As she clung to the fake rock, catching her breath, she saw that Eddie and Chelsea were still dangling from their safety ropes like giant marionettes.

Raven felt completely defeated. She was sure her friends were furious with her. "You guys," she said, "this is all my fault again. Listen, if you want to drop me as a friend, I totally understand."

"What!" cried Eddie. "You just climbed up a wall to save my butt, Rae. You don't drop friends like that."

"But I'm still going to have visions," Raven warned him.

"So what?" said Chelsea. "I mean, sure, some-times they're gonna mess us up. We're going to get mad and act like we hate you—but that's what friends do. We're not going anywhere."

"Yeah, we all got our stuff. I mean, you may not know this about me, but . . . I'm scared of heights," Eddie joked.

Dang, thought Raven, my buds are the very best in the universe. "I feel a group hug com-ing on," she told them, pushing off the wall.

Eddie caught Raven in midair. He tugged her close, then he pulled Chelsea over, and all three friends hugged.

"I love you guys!" cried Raven.

"I love you, too!" cried Chelsea.

"I'd *love* to get down!" cried Eddie.

Just then, the gym doors swung open. Vivian, Cory, and the school gym teacher rushed into the room.

"Hey, Viv!" called Raven.

"Hey, Coach!" called Eddie.

"Thought I might find you here, Cookie," said Vivian, shaking her head.

"How'd she know we were here?" asked Eddie.

"Oh, because me and Viv, we're like this," said Raven, hooking two fingers together in a "we're totally tight" gesture.

Arching one eyebrow, Cory took in the sight before his eyes. "Can't we just leave her up there?" he asked his grandmother. "This is like a dream come true."

"Keep dreamin', little man," Vivian advised him. Then she followed the coach to the safety ropes. "Come on, pull," she told Cory.

As the safety ropes finally lowered the three friends to the floor, Raven grinned.

After all our ups and downs today, we're down at last, she thought. And I am down with that!

Part Two

Part Two

Chapter One

Raven strode through the halls of Bayside, scanning every face in the crowd. She was searching for one very specific target: Gabriel Barnett.

"The Spring Dance only comes once a year," Raven told Eddie and Chelsea, who were walking with her. "And there's only one thing stopping Gabriel Barnett from asking me to the dance . . . and that's Gabriel Barnett *asking* me to the dance."

Eddie and Chelsea had heard all of this at lunch—every single day for the past week. Raven thought Gabriel was *fine*. He was tall, dark, and handsome. He had style, class, and wit. Simply put, he was the coolest hottie at

Bayside. Unfortunately, a lot of other girls thought so, too.

"There he is!" Raven finally whispered.

Gabriel stood by his locker, talking to his crew. Oh, my man is looking fine today, thought Raven. Wire-rimmed glasses framed his big brown eyes, and a Kangol cap turned backward on his head gave him an artsy yet totally stylin' look.

Raven took a deep breath. "I'm going in," she told her friends.

Raven snapped the lapels of her distressed denim jacket, struck a pose, then strutted by Gabriel with royal diva attitude.

Gabriel didn't notice.

Raven took another deep breath and tried a second pass. This time she threw in a couple of her best dance moves.

Gabriel *still* didn't notice.

Okay, thought Raven, time to take this to

Olympic level. She grabbed two gymnastic ribbons from Chelsea's gym bag and started waving them in circles. She finished her routine on one knee, then looked up, not wanting to miss Gabriel's reaction, which was . . .

Nothing. Mr. Fine and his posse just moved on down the hall toward their next class.

Raven marched over to her friends, scowling in frustration. "That's it!" she cried. "I'm through playing hard to get."

Chelsea winced. She hated to point out the obvious, but—

"Rae," she said, "he didn't even look at you."

Raven frowned. What she really needed, she decided, was a guy's advice. "Eddie, what does a girl have to do to get a guy to notice her?" she asked.

Eddie didn't seem to hear. "What is under my nail?" he muttered to himself, studying his fingers. "Hmm, I swear I don't remember eating that."

Without noticing that Raven had asked him a question, Eddie wandered off in the same direction as Gabriel.

Exasperated, Raven looked to Chelsea. What's my next move? she was about to ask. But when she opened her mouth, she nearly gagged.

A nasty smell filled the hallway. It could only be one thing.

"Stinky Sturky. Ugh!" cried Raven and Chelsea together.

As the horrific smell of Ben Sturky wafted down the hall ahead of him, kids scattered. Chelsea and Raven turned around, pretending to study a bulletin board, but it was no good. Ben walked right up to them.

"Hi, guys," he said in his usual chipper voice.

Part One

"Hey, I don't do heights, okay?"
Eddie informed Raven.

"I hate that my best friend is psychic,"
Eddie muttered.

"*These* are the ones I saw you in,"
Raven told Chelsea.

"Please tell me you just put this here,"
Chelsea said.

**"And *those* must be the 'hate me' stares,"
Raven said.**

"Your choice," Raven said.

But I *wanted* to warn you, Raven thought.

"Just stay right there!" cried Raven.

Part Two

"Hey!" cried Raven, greeting her Prince Charming.

"I hate dancing," Raven told Gabriel.

"Now, if you'll excuse me," said Cory,
"I'm due back in surgery."

"Hey, sorry I'm late!" Raven exclaimed.
"I haven't finished shaving."

"Oh, look. There's Gabriel!"
Raven exclaimed.

"To the stocks!" cried Chelsea.

"My tooth?" repeated Raven.

"Ben, speak to me!" Raven said.

Holding their breath, Raven and Chelsea turned around. Despite his body odor problem, Ben was a supersweet guy, probably the nicest boy at Bayside. The girls didn't want to be mean to him.

"Hey, Ben. Hi," they replied, discreetly covering their noses.

"So, you ladies going to the Spring Dance?" he asked. "I love spring. Everything just smells so *fresh*." Inhaling deeply, Ben raised his arms.

Nooo, thought Raven, not the armpits! But it was too late. Raven and Chelsea were instantly engulfed in a wave of stench.

"So, you guys know anybody that still doesn't have a date for the dance?" he asked.

Still reeling from the armpit assault, Raven and Chelsea couldn't shake their heads fast enough.

"'Cause Ben Sturky's looking," he said. Curving his fingers into claws, he growled like a tiger on the prowl. "Grrr . . ." And then he was gone.

Immediately, Raven and Chelsea gulped down fresh air by the bucketful.

Ben is a really nice guy, thought Raven, but a girl can only hold her breath for so long!

"Man, poor Ben," said Chelsea. "He is *so* desperate to find a date to the dance."

"Desperate is not good," Raven firmly agreed as she opened her locker. A huge photo of Gabriel "Mr. Fine" Barnett stared out from the inside of her locker door. I, myself, am not desperate, Raven told herself. When it comes to Gabriel, I'm more like enthusiastic. . . . Make that, enthusiastically *desperate*.

"Please, ask me to the dance. Please," she whispered to the photo.

Suddenly, the photo began to blur. Raven felt a familiar tingling as the world around her froze in time. . . .

Through her eye
The vision runs
Flash of future
Here it comes—

Whoa, what is up with this? I see Gabriel "Mr. Fine" Barnett wearing a velvet cape, an embroidered doublet, a feathered cap, and . . . tights?

Omigosh, I know what's up! Gabriel is in costume for the Renaissance Dance. He's dressed as Prince Charming, and—wait, wait, wait! He's opening his mouth. He's about to say something. . . .

"Rae, I've always wanted you to be my girlfriend."

When Raven came out of her vision, she thought she was going to faint. "Chelsea!" she cried, "I just saw Gabriel ask me to be his girlfriend at the Renaissance Dance. And he's going as a prince." Raven batted her eyelashes at the picture in her locker. "My prince."

"Hey, Rae," called Eddie, walking up to her. "Guess who just told me he wants to ask you to the dance?"

"Oh, I have a pretty good idea," said Raven. "And trust me, I will be ready for him."

Eddie's eyes opened wide in surprise. "Good for you," he said. "I mean, 'cause not a lot of girls would go with Stinky Sturky."

"Well, you know, that's just the kind of girl—" Raven stopped and stared as Eddie's horrifying words sank in. "I'm going *where* with *who*?"

Chapter Two

"There is no way I can DJ this dance," Eddie told Chelsea later that afternoon.

"Eddie, why not?" Chelsea whined.

"Because you picked this lame Renaissance theme!" he exclaimed, gesturing to the busy decorating going on around them. Students were filling the gym with Renaissance-era props—suits of armor, regal banners, peasant stocks, blacksmith tools, and bales of hay.

"I mean, I could've done a fifties sock hop," complained Eddie. "I could've done Motown. I would've even done country-western!" He did a little square dance two-step. "All the cowboys in the house say 'Ho!'"

"Eddie, the Elizabethan era was cool,"

Chelsea argued, "and it was exciting. You know there was dancing and jousting and juggling. . . . Plus, I'm the head of the dance committee, so that means I get to be your queen."

Chelsea walked over to the fake throne on the small raised stage and sat down. "Therefore," she said in a queenly voice, "I command you to be the DJ!"

Eddie folded his arms and glared at her.

"Please," she added in a tiny Chelsea voice.

Suddenly, they were interrupted by a freaked-out Raven. "Help me! Help me! Hide me!" she cried, sprinting into the gym. "He's coming after me! He's coming after me!"

Ben Sturky had been stalking Raven for hours. As he followed her down one hallway after another, she'd ducked from classroom to classroom and closet to closet. She'd hidden in the girls' room, under desks, behind doors . . . even on top of a row of lockers!

So far, the nasty odors had helped her stay one step ahead of Ben. But the foul-smelling boy would not give up, and Raven knew it was only a matter of time before she came face-to-face with the Sturky stink.

Now looking around the gym, Raven realized there weren't many places to hide. Spying a big bale of hay on the floor, she dove behind it. Her behind, however, didn't quite fit.

"Uh, Rae," called Eddie, "the bale's not hiding the booty."

Raven sprang up again. If my friends don't help me, she thought, I'm going to lose it. "You guys," she cried, "I have been running from Ben all day!"

"You know, Rae," said Chelsea, "if he asked you, you could just say 'no.'"

Raven sighed. "I know, but he's such a sweet guy. I don't want to hurt his feelings. Besides, I just want Gabriel to ask me first so I can say, 'Gee, Ben I'm sorry, but I already have a date for the dance.'"

"Oh," said Chelsea, scratching her head in confusion. "So, Gabriel takes you to the dance, he asks you to be his girlfriend, and then your vision comes true?"

"Now, I wasn't thinking that far ahead," Raven confessed. With her entire afternoon spent hiding from Stinky Sturky, she'd had precious few minutes to daydream about her vision of Gabriel. "But," she admitted to Chelsea, "that sounds good to me!"

Just then, Raven froze. But it wasn't because she was having another vision. Something reeked. Her nose wrinkled up and she gagged.

"He's a hundred feet and closing," she told her friends. By now, she'd gotten her Stinky

Sturky dodges down to a science. "I still have time to escape."

Raven raced to the door, then skidded to a stop. The smell was so overwhelming she knew it was too late to run. I am totally busted, she realized, spinning on her heels. As Ben approached the gym, Raven plastered herself against the wall right next to the entrance.

Ben strode into the gym and Raven lunged for the doorway, ready to slip out behind him. But the entrance was blocked by kids carrying big banners.

No place to hide! Raven thought.

Her only chance now was to shadow Ben's every move. As he walked farther into the gym, Raven stuck close behind him, praying he wouldn't make any sudden turns.

"Did I just see Raven come in here?" Ben asked Chelsea and Eddie.

Chelsea nervously shook her head and

shrugged. Eddie was even less convincing. "I have not seen Raven anywhere," he said stiffly.

Raven rolled her eyes. It's a good thing Ben is a gullible guy, she thought.

"It's funny, I feel like I just keep missing her," Ben told them. He paused a moment, looked to his right, then to his left. Raven ducked just in time to avoid being seen.

"All right," Ben finally said, "well . . . see ya."

Without warning, Ben lifted his arm to wave good-bye, and Raven was struck by a wall of stink. As Ben raced away, she collapsed onto the hay bale behind her.

Just then, Gabriel walked in. When she spotted him, Raven quickly struck a pose, transforming herself from pitiful stench victim to chic supermodel in record time.

"Hay," Gabriel said, staring at her.

"Hey!" cried Raven, greeting her Prince

Charming with a sugar-sweet grin. Dreamy-eyed, she waved.

"Uh, no," he said, frowning. He pointed to her head. "Hay. Stuck in your hair."

Raven tittered nervously as he walked off. Then, she slumped back on the hay bale, embarrassed.

Way to keep it real, Rae, she told herself. As in, real *country*.

"Look, there's Gabriel," Raven whispered to Chelsea an hour later. They were standing in the doorway of their next class. Gabriel was sitting alone at a table in the art room, examining his camera.

Things haven't gone very well so far, Raven told herself, but the day is not over yet!

"Okay," she told Chelsea, "if my vision's going to come true, I've got to get him to ask me to that dance."

As Chelsea headed to her seat, Raven crossed the room to sit at Gabriel's table. "Hey, Gabriel, nice camera," she said. The art teacher had asked everyone to bring in a camera so they could begin their study of photography.

"Oh, this?" said Gabriel, waving his hand. "Aw, it's just a multizone auto-focus with a 200-millimeter zoom lens."

Right, thought Raven. She pulled out her own camera. What can you say about a disposable camera? she wondered.

"I can throw mine away," she told Gabriel, tossing it over her shoulder. Chelsea caught it, and Raven laughed uncomfortably.

Click! Click! Click!

Before she knew it, Gabriel had focused his fancy camera lens on her face and snapped her photo like a pro.

"Nice picture," he said.

"But I wasn't even ready," Raven protested.

"Oh, but those are the best ones," Gabriel replied. "You see, I like things that are spontaneous."

"You do?" Raven asked, smiling. He'd just handed her the *perfect* set up. "Well, you know, there's a *dance* tomorrow night," she hinted coyly.

Gabriel looked away. "Yeah, I know, but I'm not going."

"Oh, me neither," she quickly agreed. "Isn't that funny? You're not going. I'm not going." Raven bit her lip. She just couldn't leave it at that. "How come you're not going?"

"I'm not really into dancing," he told her flatly.

"I hate dancing," Raven echoed.

Gabriel's eyebrows knitted together in confusion. He pointed at her chest. "But your shirt says, 'Loves to dance.'"

Raven frowned, suddenly remembering which shirt she was wearing—the same one she'd spent hours sewing sequins onto the night before so Gabriel wouldn't miss the hint.

"Well, I'm wearing this shirt because, um . . ." She pointed at Chelsea who was watching them from a few seats away. "I borrowed it from her. She's a dancing fool."

"Yeah, I'm just a dancing fool," Chelsea called, trying to help out her best friend.

Then she jumped to her feet and started to dance. Now I know why Chelsea suggested a Renaissance theme for the Spring Dance, Raven thought, watching her. Her moves belong in the history books!

"Stop dancing, fool," Raven hissed.

"I don't even know why they have these spring dances," Gabriel complained. "I mean, nobody even dances."

"But they're good for a lot of different things," Raven replied. "I mean, people talk, socialize . . . *relationships* are formed. . . ."

Hint, hint, she thought in exasperation. What in the world will it take for this boy to get the message? she wondered. A halftime show with cheerleaders holding letters that spell out ASK RAVEN TO THE DANCE?

"You know what?" asked Gabriel.

"I'd love to," Raven blurted out.

"Great," said Gabriel, "because . . . you're in *Riley's* seat."

Raven looked up to find Riley standing next to her, waiting for her to get up. "Right," said Raven, disappointed again.

Slowly, she rose and Riley sat down. Raven dejectedly dragged herself over to the art table where Chelsea was sitting.

"He is so wrong, Rae," Chelsea whispered indignantly.

Raven sighed and nodded. At least Chelsea understands, she thought. Just then, Chelsea pointed to Riley and added, "That's *Matthew*'s seat."

Raven just shook her head.

Chapter Three

"**U**h, Rae, I don't know about this petticoat," Chelsea complained, checking herself out in the mirror. "It doesn't seem very . . . royal."

With pins in her mouth, Raven sat on a stool in her attic bedroom, fitting Chelsea into her Renaissance costume.

"Well," said Raven, taking the pins out of her mouth, "unless the queen wants a royal pin stuck in her royal butt, she better be royally quiet. Okay?"

"So, Rae," said Eddie, who was chilling on a chair nearby. "Do you think you'd go to the dance with Ben if he didn't smell?"

"Honestly, no," said Raven. "I mean, he's a nice guy, but unless he took a shower and came out as Gabriel, it ain't there for me."

"Well, you can't just hide from him forever," Chelsea told her.

"Girl, I don't need forever, okay?" said Raven. "I just need enough time for my future boyfriend to ask me to the dance."

"Rae," said Eddie, "I've been kind of, sort of holding this back because I knew how you'd feel. . . ." He paused and sighed.

Uh-oh, thought Raven, recognizing Eddie's Bad News sigh. She held her breath and waited.

"I heard that Gabriel is taking Rachel to the dance," Eddie confessed.

That's not bad news, Raven thought. That's a full-on tragedy. "Really?" she asked Eddie, her hopes collapsing.

He nodded.

"Oh, Rae, I'm sorry," said Chelsea.

Just then, Raven's little brother walked into

the room and announced, "Hey, Raven, your stinky boyfriend is here."

And the bad news just keeps on coming, Raven thought. "Oh, no. Ben found me," she said.

"At your own house," Cory said sarcastically. "Imagine that."

Raven sighed and turned to her brother. "Cory, I need you to get rid of him for me."

"Too bad some guys just can't read women," Cory said. "If a girl doesn't like you, she doesn't like you. But if she likes you, you know it." He strutted over to Chelsea. "Ain't that right, baby?" he asked, grinning at her.

Chelsea shrank back in horror. "Be gone," she ordered in her Don't Mess With Queen Chelsea voice.

"Okay," said Cory. "But I'll be back." Then he turned to his big sister. "Leave him to me. I'll let him down easy," he promised.

Raven watched Cory go. After a minute, she rose from her stool and headed for the door. She didn't trust Cory to be sensitive. Not one bit.

Sure enough, Raven found Cory at the front door, wearing a blue surgical mask to block the smell of Ben Sturky's body odor.

Ben didn't seem to care though. He looked excited and happy to be standing inside Raven's house. Until Cory said, "Raven told me to tell you she's *not* hiding upstairs in her bedroom."

Ben's face fell. "Got it," he said.

From the top of the stairs, Raven heard the hurt in Ben's voice. She felt horrible.

"Now, if you'll excuse me," said Cory, raising his hands straight up like an O.R. physician. "I'm due back in surgery."

"Tell your sister I get the message," Ben said sadly.

"Hey, Ben?" Raven called, rushing down the stairs.

Ben moved quickly toward the front door. "Um, that's okay," he told Raven. "Your brother made things pretty clear."

My brother is lower than a mud-bellied snake, Raven wanted to tell him, and I can't let you leave like this. "Hey, Ben," she found herself saying instead, "how would you like to go to the dance with me?"

Ben whipped around in surprise. "You want to go with me?" he asked, stunned.

"Why not?" said Raven. "I mean, you don't have a date, I definitely don't have a date, and now we do."

"Really?" A goofy grin spread across Ben's face. "Score!" he cried. "I'll pick you up at seven. No, uh, me and *my mom* will pick you up," he corrected himself—as if having his mother along was a *good* thing.

Raven shook her head. The poor, clueless stinker, she thought. Then she realized: dang, now he's *my* poor, clueless stinker.

"Rae, what did you just do?" Chelsea asked, rushing down the steps in alarm.

"Look, he's a nice guy, and he wants to go with me," said Raven with a shrug. "Besides, I'm not going with the guy I want to go with anyway, so what's the big deal?"

Just then, the phone rang.

"Hello?" said Raven. Her jaw dropped when she recognized the voice on the other end of the line. "Hi, Gabriel," she said. "What? You want to go to the dance? With me?"

Now Chelsea's jaw dropped. "What?" she whispered. "You're going with Ben!"

Raven scowled and pressed her fingertips together, telling Chelsea to shush.

"But I kind of heard that you were going with Rachel," Raven told Gabriel. "It ain't true, huh?" She glared at Eddie, who shrugged in apology.

"Look, Gabriel," said Raven finally, "it's really sweet of you to ask me to the dance, but . . ."

Chelsea gave Raven a sympathetic look. Doing the right thing was always tough, but Chelsea was sure Raven would tell Gabriel that she already had a date with Stinky—but very sweet—Sturky.

"I'd love to go!" Raven blurted. "Okay, bye!" She hung up the phone. "What?" she asked when she saw Chelsea and Eddie frowning at her.

With a defensive shrug, Raven simply pointed to the sparkles on her T-shirt and said, "I love to dance."

Chapter Four

By the day of the dance, Raven still hadn't figured out how to get out of her date with Ben Sturky. She decided she needed an expert's advice. So Raven sought out the one person she knew was a master in deception—her little brother, Cory.

"The only way I am going to get out of this date with Ben is for him to find me disgusting and repulsive," she told Cory, stepping closer and closer to him with every word.

Cory shrank back in his chair. "Have you tried standing this close to him?" he asked.

Okay, Raven admitted to herself, I'm getting a little intense here. With a sigh, she took two steps back.

"Look," she told her brother. "I don't want to hurt Ben's feelings, so the only way to solve my two-date problem is to get him to dump me."

"Well, let me just pull out my 'What's Disgusting About Raven' file," Cory said, reaching under the desk. He lifted a cardboard box filled with files and placed it on the desktop.

"You have a *file* on that?" Raven asked.

Cory laughed as he rifled through the dozens of files in the box. "Let's start with the A's, shall we?" he said.

Raven couldn't believe it. "You have it *alphabetical*?"

"Alphabetical, by date, by location, and by body part," said Cory flatly. "How do you want it?"

Raven's eyes narrowed. "Surprise me," she said.

Cory selected a file and opened it. "Okay, body parts," he began. "You clip your toenails at the kitchen table."

"I do not!" Raven cried.

"You blow your nose and then look in the tissue," Cory continued.

Ooh, she thought, the maggot has got me there. "That was *once*," she admitted, "and it was a *surprising* color."

"You could make a wig from all the hair you leave in the shower drain," Cory went on.

"Okay, now, *that* is ridiculous," snapped Raven.

Cory's reply was to pull a scraggly looking wig from the file box. Raven shuddered in disgust.

That's my hair all right, she thought. And I bet there's just enough to make a rope long enough to strangle Cory with.

"The truth isn't pretty, my friend," said Cory.

Ding-dong!

"Okay, look, that's Ben," Raven said, hearing the doorbell. "I'm going to go upstairs and get ready. You let him in and start making me look bad."

Cory smiled smugly. "A job I was born to do," he declared.

Downstairs, Cory opened the front door to find Ben Sturky clad head-to-toe in a shiny silver suit of armor.

"I'm here to fetch fair Raven," Ben announced gallantly.

Waving Ben inside, Cory began Plan A, also known as Operation Repulsive. "She's deciding whether she can get away with wearing the same underwear three days in a row," he told Ben. "Come in."

Ben frowned, but he failed to turn tail and run for the hills. Instead, he took a step inside.

Cory frowned, too. *Guess I'll try another*

pitch, he told himself. "So, I see you're wearing armor," he noted. "Smart man."

"What do you mean?" asked Ben.

"Have you ever seen Raven eat? She's like a blender without the lid! Brrrrr—blech!" Cory cried, flailing his arms and pretending to chew up and spew out food in all directions.

Ben frowned at that one, too. But he continued to wait patiently. Just then, Raven came tramping down the stairs, wearing a ratty bathrobe. Her head was wrapped in an old scarf, and her jaw and chin were covered with shaving cream.

"Hey, sorry I'm late!" she exclaimed, rushing up to Ben. "I haven't finished shaving. Oh, nice suit—" Seeing her reflection in his armor, she began to use it like a shaving mirror.

"You shave?" asked Ben, watching Raven whip a razor this way and that across her jaw.

"Oh, yeah," said Raven. "But if you don't

want to be seen with me, I'll completely understand."

"Oh, no, Raven," Ben replied sincerely. "I care about what's on the *inside*."

"Oh, you do?" Raven said with disappointment. "Oh, that's great." Whoa, she thought, this guy is going to be tough to gross out! Taking a deep breath, she tried again—

"Well, could you help me out? Look in here." Tilting her head back, Raven lifted the tip of her nose and showed Ben her nostrils. "Is there a bat in the cave?"

"No, try me!" Ben cried, tipping his head back, too.

Raven recoiled. If I keep this up, she realized, Ben is likely to take this repulsive thing to a whole new level. Better quit while I'm ahead, she decided, and move on to Plan B— which *better* not stand for *busted*.

Chapter Five

The Bayside Renaissance Dance was in full swing. At the entrance to the gym, trumpeters heralded the arrival of each guest. Colorful banners hung on the walls. All around the gym, suits of armor, royal shields, and other period props helped transform the basketball court into an old English court.

On a stage decorated to look like a castle turret, Eddie was spinning records dressed as the Hunchback of Notre Dame—hump and all. Sitting on her throne nearby, wearing petticoats, pearls, and some royal attitude, was Queen Chelsea.

"Dance, peasants, dance!" she commanded, getting into her role.

When Chelsea saw Ben and Raven enter the gym, she rushed over to greet them. "Welcome to my very merry feast, sir knight and . . ." She stopped to take a closer look at Raven. "Ugly hag?"

Raven had dressed as an old beggar-woman in a patch-covered burlap cape. She also wore a scruffy wig, a fake crooked nose, a wart-covered chin, and a blackened tooth. Despite her repulsive costume, Ben stood next to her, beaming.

Raven turned to him. "Hey, Ben, would you mind getting me some punch?" she asked.

"Oh, we *haveth* no punch," Chelsea jumped in. "Only grog."

"Fine. Diet grog. Grog. I don't care," Raven snapped impatiently. "Just grog me, okay. Thank you."

When Ben left, Chelsea leaned toward Raven. "Well, at least he doesn't smell tonight," she whispered.

"Girl, it must be that armor," Raven agreed. "The stink is sealed in there like a can of tuna."

Just then, Raven spotted her Prince Charming entering the gym. "Oh, look. There's Gabriel," she said dreamily.

Chelsea frowned at Raven's ugly hag costume. "You cannot let him see you like that," she said.

Raven waved her hand. "Girl, you know I got it covered. Please." Then she turned her cape inside out, instantly transforming from a homely peasant into a fair maiden. She plucked off her fake nose and chin, removed her black tooth, and dropped them all into her bag.

"All right, all right, all right!" cried Eddie from his DJ turret. "This one here goes out to all the pretty ladies in the castle. Tonight we're going to party like it's 1599!"

The crowd in the gym was ready for Eddie

to rock the house. Then the music began—a gloomy lute piece from Chelsea's *Renaissance Greatest Hits* CD.

The kids groaned.

Chelsea crossed over to Eddie, who stepped down off his DJ turret. "Eddie, no one's dancing," she said, concerned.

"*You* try to get a groove going with the music you gave me," he complained.

"Edward, do not question your queen!" cried Chelsea. "Now, return to your Castle of Funk and get thee jiggy with it!"

Eddie rolled his eyes. "You got problems," he told her.

Meanwhile, on the other side of the gym, fair maiden Raven swept up to Gabriel. Her chiffon gown flowed around her like a lilac-colored cloud, and her sleek dark hair had been artfully braided with purple ribbons.

"Wow," Gabriel told her. "If I knew you

were going to get so dressed up, I would've worn pants."

Raven laughed and asked, "So, what are you supposed to be? Prince Charming or something?"

"Actually, Charming was taken. So you're stuck with Prince Congeniality," he joked. "I'm not really charming, but I'm popular around the castle."

Raven laughed again. She just *loved* Gabriel's wit. "I could listen to you forever," she said with a dreamy sigh.

Just then, Raven noticed Ben returning with her diet grog. She turned back to Gabriel. "But not right now, okay?" she blurted out. "Hey, eat, drink, be merry. Love me. Miss me. Okay." Then she pushed her charming prince toward one of the refreshment tables and rushed off to meet her stinky knight.

With a flip of her hooded cape and a quick

application of the pointy chin, crooked nose, and black tooth, Raven transformed herself back into an ugly hag. She hurried toward Ben, passing Chelsea's throne on her way.

A juggler had been attempting to amuse Queen Chelsea. When Raven rushed past, however, he dropped one of his juggling pins.

"Jester, you have displeased me!" cried Chelsea. She pointed a bejeweled finger to a corner of the gym. "To the stocks!"

Students dressed as dungeon masters grabbed the juggler—who was really their principal, Mr. Lawler—and escorted him away.

Wow, thought Raven, Chelsea's actually sending the principal to the stocks. Could it be that she's taking this whole queen thing just a little *too* seriously?

But Raven didn't have time to worry about Chelsea. She had her own problems!

"Let's dance, okay?" Ben told Raven excitedly when he met up with her again. "It may be kind of hard in this," he explained, gesturing to his armor, "but I can take it off."

"No!" cried every student within hearing—and smelling—distance. Raven had to agree. For all our sake, Raven silently vowed, I will not allow Ben to break that seal!

With a shrug, Ben put on his helmet. Then Eddie put on a new record—one from a more *recent* century—and a funky beat pounded through the sound system. The kids cheered and rushed onto the dance floor.

Suddenly, the music scratched to a halt. Queen Chelsea had turned it off.

"What?" cried Eddie in disbelief. "They were finally dancing!"

"Your queen is not amused," Chelsea complained. "We need the classics."

"Well, it's Motown," Eddie pointed out.

Come on, he thought, you can't get any more classic than that!

"I want something more like this," said Chelsea. She grabbed the microphone and began to sing a sixteenth-century ballad.

The students stared at Chelsea for a second, unable to believe their ears. Then everyone began to throw vegetables and fruit at her.

"Protect your queen!" shrieked Chelsea, grabbing a girl in a peasant costume and using her as a human shield. "Protect your queen!"

While Chelsea was distracted by flying produce, Eddie slipped on a pair of sunglasses and a new CD. Once again, dance music filled the gym.

The students sent up a cheer and resumed their dancing. Raven and Ben began to dance, too.

Suddenly, Raven noticed Gabriel at the other end of the dance floor. Okay, she told herself, think fast. I have to find a way to keep Ben from seeing me with Gabriel.

Reaching up, Raven flipped down the visor on Ben's helmet.

"I can't see," complained Ben, his head darting this way and that.

"Oh, well then just *feel* the music," Raven advised him. And with that, she swiftly danced away.

Chapter Six

After another quick change, fair maiden Raven danced over to her Prince Charming.

"So," she said to Gabriel with a flirty smile, "there's something you wanted to tell me?"

"Yeah, um," he said, staring at her mouth. "What's that on your tooth?"

"My tooth?" repeated Raven. Suddenly she realized she'd forgotten to remove her blackened hag tooth. "My tooth. Right. Well, actually, the tooth is—" Totally fake! she wanted to scream.

As Raven spun around to remove the fake tooth, she accidentally bumped into Queen Chelsea.

"Well, you've managed to bump the royal

heinie," said Chelsea, outraged. She pointed toward the corner of the gym. "To the stocks!"

"Chelsea?" Raven cried in disbelief.

"To the stocks!" Chelsea insisted. A moment later, two dungeon masters grabbed Raven's arms and pulled her away.

"Chelsea!" Raven cried.

"Now, to the stocks," Chelsea insisted.

"Chelsea no. Chelsea stop!" begged Raven.

But it did no good. The dungeon masters escorted Raven to the fake stocks, where Mr. Lawler was still imprisoned.

"Just p-play along and accep-pt your p-punishment," the principal advised, spraying saliva with every "p."

Raven bent over as her head and hands were locked into the stocks.

Just then, Eddie wandered over. "So," he said, "how are things going with Prince Charming and Sir Stink-a-lot?"

"Not good, okay?" snapped Raven, struggling to twist her head to see Eddie. "Gabriel hasn't asked me to be his girlfriend. Ben hasn't dumped me. And my best friend just put me in the stocks!" She frowned and beckoned Eddie closer. "C'mere," she said, thinking, *let me break it down for you.* "I'm psychic, and I didn't see this coming!"

"Okay, so how long do you think you can keep this up?" Eddie asked.

"Just long enough for Gabriel and I to have some alone time," said Raven. "But for some reason Ben keeps hanging around me."

For *some* reason? Eddie looked at her in disbelief. "I don't know, Rae," he said, crossing his arms, "maybe it's because he's your *date.*"

"Oh, look, look!" Raven cried, staring across the room. "Gabriel's going into the hall. This is my chance," she told Eddie.

Raven struggled inside the fake stocks. "I've

got to get out of here, Eddie," she cried, trying to pull her wrists and head free. But the painted plywood wouldn't give. "I can't get out of here!" she wailed.

"It's locked, Rae. It's locked," Eddie tried to tell her. He examined the lock to see if he could open it, but he wasn't fast enough for Raven.

"There's no time!" she cried, struggling with all her might. *Crack!* Raven broke the stocks and pulled free of the platform. Unfortunately, her head and wrists remained clamped in the plywood.

At least I can move now, Raven thought as she stumbled across the gym. She had to turn this way and that to avoid smacking people as she passed.

At that moment, Queen Chelsea declared from her throne, "Let the jousting begin!"

Uh-oh, Raven thought as knights on fake

horses charged from the corners of the room. I think I'm in the middle of the jousting field!

As the two knights ran toward one another, Raven was trapped. With each pass, the knights rudely slammed the ends of her stocks, spinning her like a top.

Finally, Raven had had enough. Time to *join* this joust, she decided. Using her plywood stocks, Raven took both knights out on the next pass. *Crash! Bang!* She watched them go flying. And don't stop till you get to the sixteenth century! she silently wailed.

Must. Get. To. Gabriel, Raven chanted to herself as she raced toward the door. But when she tried to barrel through it, the ends of the long stocks slammed against the doorframe. *Bam!* She bounced backward. *Bam! Bam! Bam!* She tried again and again, but her stocks were simply too wide to fit through.

Finally, Raven stopped. Okay, she thought,

did I not learn shapes in preschool? Turning sideways, she was able to fit through the door.

Raven ran down the hall, searching for Gabriel. Finally, she heard his voice coming from just around the corner.

"Rae? Rae?"

He's calling me! Raven thought. Joyfully, she took a few more steps—then stopped dead.

"Rachel. Just stop and talk to me!" Gabriel cried.

Rachel, thought Raven. *Oh, no.*

She heard Rachel snap angrily, "What?"

Raven peeked around the corner. Sure enough, Gabriel was standing in the hallway. He looked just like he did in her vision: tall, dark, and Prince Charming handsome.

"Rachel," Gabriel said to the pretty girl standing in front him, "I really wanted to come to the dance with you."

"Then why are you here with Raven Baxter?" asked Rachel, clearly annoyed.

"Because you said yes to Jarrod," Gabriel replied. "And Raven's been dropping hints all week. Look, she's a nice girl, and she really wanted to go with me. I felt bad for her, so I just asked her to the dance. It's no big deal."

"Do you like her?" Rachel asked.

"No," Gabriel insisted. "Look, it's just a pity date. It doesn't mean anything . . . Rae, I've always wanted you to be my girlfriend."

Raven shut her eyes. Finally, she understood. Those were the exact words Gabriel had said in her vision—but the Rae he had in mind hadn't been Raven. It had been Rachel.

Devastated, Raven turned and ran back into the gym. She went straight to Eddie and told him everything.

"I can't believe this," she said, as Eddie finally helped her out of the stocks. "Gabriel took me to the dance because he felt sorry for me. A pity date. I mean, how could he do this? I really liked this guy. How could he do that to me?"

"Sort of like what you did to Ben?" Eddie quietly pointed out.

Raven hadn't thought it was possible to feel any worse. But now she did.

"Yeah. Right," she admitted.

Raven realized she needed to set things straight. Looking around the gym, she saw Ben's familiar silver suit of armor standing by the refreshment table. She left Eddie and walked over to him.

Reluctantly, she sidled up to the back of his armor. "Hey, Ben," she said sadly. "I've got to tell you something and it's really hard to say, so I'm just going to say it. I shouldn't have asked you to the dance. I mean, the only reason I did was because I knew you liked me, and I thought if I asked you it would be nice, and

I guess it wasn't really very nice, was it? Ben, I'm really, really sorry. Ben?"

Raven waited for Ben to react. But he just stood there, not moving a muscle—or a metal plate. Not even a rivet!

"I know this is hard to hear, but Ben, say something," Raven coaxed. Still, he didn't say a word. Now Raven was getting worried. Was he crying? Was he furious beyond words? "Ben, speak to me!"

Raven reached to lift up his helmet's visor . . . and his entire head fell off! Raven almost screamed, but a voice stopped her.

"Wow."

Raven turned to find the real Ben Sturky standing right behind her. He was still wearing his suit of armor. Raven suddenly realized she'd been talking to a prop!

"Um, how much of that did you hear?" Raven asked Ben.

"Well, unless there was a good part, all of it," said Ben. He sounded monumentally crushed.

"Ben, I really want us to be friends," Raven quickly told him. "That's good, right?" When he didn't reply, Raven winced and said, "You hate me, don't you."

Ben sighed, then admitted, "I could never hate you." He gestured to the headless knight. "*He* might hate you, but I never could."

That is *so* sweet, thought Raven. "So, um, you still need a date to the dance?" she asked.

With a sigh, Ben offered his arm. Raven took it. "C'mon, m'lady," he said.

As they crossed the dance floor, Ben added, "I mean, you know, it could have been worse. You could have been here with another guy."

Uh, right, thought Raven, wincing again. But let's not go there.

Just then, a crowd of enraged peasants rushed past them, carrying Queen Chelsea toward the gym doors. Eddie was right on the group's heels.

"You don't know who you're dealing with!" shrieked Chelsea. "I am your queen! Eddie, tell them!"

But Eddie was nobody's fool. "Off with her head!" he howled.

Dang, thought Raven, looks like Queen Chelsea is finally getting what she deserves—a royal bouncing.

Later that night, Raven lay in bed, exhausted but unable to sleep.

The day had been hard, and she had a lot to think about, but that wasn't what was keeping her awake. It was something much more distressing—namely, her little brother.

Now that Cory had started giving Raven examples from his "What's Disgusting About Raven" file, he wouldn't stop!

". . . you've got that mole on your foot that looks like an extra toe," he read aloud, pacing back and forth next to her bed.

"It's over, Cory," Raven moaned for the tenth time.

But Cory ignored her. "The only thing that grows faster than the hair on your head," he read, "is the hair on your lip."

That's it! Raven thought. In one fluid motion she sat up, grabbed the biggest pillow on her bed, and flung it in Cory's direction. *Bam!* She knocked him to the floor, where he blinked at her in stunned surprise.

Raven smiled. This wasn't exactly a fairy tale day, she thought. But at least it had a happy ending!

Gaze into the future and take a sneak peek at the next *That's So Raven* story. . . .

Adapted by Jasmine Jones
Based on the series created by
Michael Poryes
Susan Sherman
Based on the teleplay written by
Beth Seriff & Geoff Tarson

Why do they have to make the hallways so depressing? Raven Baxter wondered, as she and her best friend, Chelsea Daniels, walked down the crowded, dingy school corridor.

Raven cast an eye over the drab olive-colored walls and gray lockers. A few posters announcing the Student Council elections hung on the walls. I mean, it's bad enough that we have to be at school at all, she thought. They don't need to throw salt on the wound.

"Please, Rae. It doesn't matter who wins the Student Council elections," Chelsea said, continuing the conversation they'd been having. "The president never gets anything done. We need a president who'll actually do something, you know? I mean, this place is falling apart."

The girls stopped at their lockers. Chelsea spun her combination and yanked at her locker door. It didn't budge.

"It's not that bad," Raven protested, yanking at her own locker. It didn't open, either. Raven shot Chelsea a knowing look. They'd been through this routine before—about five thousand times.

"Uno, dos, tres," Raven and Chelsea counted in unison. Raven whacked the wall to the left of the row of lockers as Chelsea did the same on the right. Once, twice, three times—then they kicked the bottom row of lockers. Simultaneously, all of the lockers in the row popped open, revealing everything inside.

Hmm, Raven thought, as she peered at the collage of magazine photos taped inside the door of another locker. I didn't know Jimmy was so into the U.S. Women's Beach Volleyball team. And Gina—man, she's got some suspicious stuff in here. Like, why would she need two copies of our history book? Makes you wonder . . .

Chelsea frowned in disgust. "And Rae, look at these lockers," she said.

"Yeah, I know," Raven agreed. "It's horrible the way they just open up like that." She peeked into another locker and her eyes widened. Pay dirt! "Oh, girl, look! The new Mary J. Blige CD. I gotta borrow this one," she said, pulling it out and shoving it into her own locker.

Chelsea glared at her.

Guiltily, Raven put the CD back into the locker she'd taken it from. I was just going to borrow it, she thought defensively. I would have put it back . . . you know, eventually. If I remembered.

"Rae, you know, it would be so easy to get them fixed." Chelsea shut all of the other lockers, then dug around in her own locker for her books. "All you have to do is write a letter to the school maintenance department. It's right there in section G-42 of the student manual."

Raven looked at her. "There's a student manual?"

Chelsea rolled her eyes and slammed her locker shut.

Automatically, Raven and Chelsea held their notebooks over their heads as plaster rained down from the ceiling.

Oh, snap, Raven thought as she brushed it off the shoulders of her blue velvet duster. I *hate* looking like I've got plaster dandruff.

"Girl, you should just run," Raven said as she and Chelsea headed down the hall.

"Rae, there's no running in the school halls," Chelsea replied. "Section I-19. Hallway do's and don'ts," she added chirpily.

Raven gave her friend a look. "I *meant* you should run for student president," she explained. "'Do's and don'ts,'" she muttered to herself in disgust. I swear, Chelsea *looks* normal, Raven thought, eyeing her friend's striped sweater, jeans, and the sparkly barrettes in her red hair. But do normal people memorize whole sections of the student manual?

"I don't know, Rae," Chelsea said. "I'm not the kind of person people vote for. You know, you've got to be in the 'in crowd.'" Chelsea made air quotes around the words. "And who wants that?"

"Yeah," Raven agreed, then added under her breath, "I do."

"I don't know," Chelsea said again. "I mean, I know I'd be a really good president, but—"

Raven cut her off. "But what? Chelsea, you know about all the problems." Just then, a foul odor wafted past Raven's nose. Ooh, now the atmosphere around here is *really* getting putrid, Raven thought. "And when you get elected," she added, "could you do something about that stench?"

It took a moment for Raven and Chelsea to realize that that was no ordinary stench. It was so foul, so pungent, so brain-scramblingly disgusting that it could only be one thing . . .

"Ben Sturky!" Raven and Chelsea cried.

They tried to run, but Stinky Sturky charged right past them. He stopped dead in front of the Student Council elections sign-up poster.

While his back was turned, Raven and Chelsea tried desperately to fan the stench away. Ben was a sweet guy, but he definitely didn't smell like it.

A moment later, Ben whipped around to face them. Raven and Chelsea pretended to be fanning themselves. But Ben didn't seem to notice anything out of the ordinary.

"Student Council elections," he said with a hungry gleam in his eye. "I think I'm going to run. I smell victory."

"Oh, we all do," Raven assured him, trying to breathe through her mouth. "I'm sure everybody does."

"Thanks!" Ben said brightly. "Rock the vote."

"How about 'wash' the vote?" Chelsea whispered to Raven as Ben hurried off down the hall.

Or deodorize the vote, Raven thought.

"You know, Rae," Chelsea said thoughtfully as she fell into step beside Raven, "I was thinking, I wouldn't be that bad at it." She hugged her books against her chest. "I could be a really good president. You know, I'm friendly, I'm loyal, I'm energetic. . . ." Chelsea stopped in her tracks. "I just described a dog, didn't I?"

Raven bit her lip. "Yeah," she admitted. "But, you know, people love dogs." She put her hand on Chelsea's shoulder. "Think about it, Chels. You against Ben Sturky. You do the math."

Suddenly, Raven's hand went cold. The world around her began to spin. . . .

**Through her eye
The vision runs
Flash of future
Here it comes—**

What's this? I'm seeing a poster with the names BEN STURKY *and* CHELSEA DANIELS *written on it.*

Hey, check it out—it's the results of the Student Council election! Looks like Ben got 187 votes. Who knew he was so popular?

Wait, wait! Now the number of votes for Chelsea is coming into focus. It looks like she got . . . 3?

Oh, no!

My girl's gonna lose—to Stinky Sturky!

A moment later, Raven came out of her vision. She swallowed hard and glanced guiltily at her best friend. I just told Chelsea to do the math about beating Ben, Raven realized, but that equation doesn't add up the way I thought it would.

"Actually, math wasn't my very best subject," Raven mumbled quickly.

"Okay, Rae." Chelsea grinned, clenching her fists in excitement. "I wanna do it. You totally convinced me. I want to run. Oh, I never would have thought about doing this if it wasn't for you. Thank you." She gave Raven a huge hug.

Raven felt like she couldn't breathe—and it wasn't just because of Chelsea's squeeze. How can I tell her that she's going to lose by 184 votes? Raven thought. It would hurt her feelings too much.

Okay, Raven decided, when in doubt, fake it. "Yeah, girl," Raven said uneasily. "What are friends for?"

Chelsea gave a quick wave and hurried

off down the hall. Raven watched her go.

She's so happy, Raven thought. So excited. So gung-ho . . .

How in the world am I going to get out of this one? Raven wondered miserably.

FIRST TIME ON DVD AND VIDEO

Sassy, Stylish and Psychic!

FEATURES
NEVER-BEFORE-SEEN
EPISODE

that's so raven

Supernaturally Stylish

COMING DECEMBER 7

Get Cheetah Power!

the Cheetah Girls

Includes An
Alternate Ending
& Exclusive
Behind-The-Scenes
Look

Now on DVD and Video

Groove to the sound of all your favorite shows

Disney Channel Soundtrack Series

Disney's
Kim Possible
TV Soundtrack

The Cheetah Girls
TV Soundtrack

Lizzie McGuire
TV Soundtrack

Pixel Perfect
Soundtrack

Also, look for...

- **The Proud Family TV Series Soundtrack**
- **That's So Raven TV Series Soundtrack**

Collect them all!